CAT TRIVIA

FUN Q & A
FOR CAT LOVERS

Introduction

How well do you know your cat? This book is full of fun trivia about cats. You can either read for fun or quizz your friends or family on how well they know their furry friends.

How to read or play?

Play to win or read for fun, the choice is yours!
To play for fun, all you need to do is read through the questions and see if you know the answers. It can also be great fun to read the questions out to family or friends, and see who knows the most about cats.

If you want to play to win, pick either 10 to 15 questions each. You get 1 point for each correct answer. The winner is the person with the most points.

Where are the answers?

For each set of questions, the answers are located on the reverse of the page. There are two answers per page (1 top and 1 bottom), so try to cover the answers to the questions you have not seen.

Q1. Cats are the only mammals who cannot taste what?

 QUESTIONS

Q2. Are cats near-sighted or farsighted?

A1. Sweetness

 ANSWERS

A2. Near-sighted

Q3. How many toes does a cat have?

 QUESTIONS

Q4. How many times their length can a cat jump?

A3. 18 toes

 ANSWERS

A4. 6 times

Q5. How many bones does a cat have?

 QUESTIONS

Q6. How many more bones does a cat have than a human?

A5. 230 bones

 ANSWERS

A6. 24 bones

Q7. What is the name of Geppetto's cat in Pinocchio?

 QUESTIONS

Q8. Are male cats more likely to be left-pawed or right-pawed?

A7. Figaro

 ANSWERS

A8. Left-pawed

Q9. On average, cats typically sleep more than how many hours a day?

 QUESTIONS

Q10. What portion of its waking hours can a cat spend on grooming?

A9. 12 hours

 ANSWERS

A10. A third

Q11. Despite popular belief, many cats are actually intolerant to what?

Q12. From what age can a female cat get pregnant?

A11. Lactose

 ANSWERS

A12. 4 months old

Q13. Neutered male cats on average live what percentage longer than unneutered cats?

 QUESTIONS

Q14. A cat's grooming process stimulates the flow of what to the skin?

A13. 60 percent

 ANSWERS

A14. Blood

Q15. If a cat has a question-marked shaped tail, it is asking you to do what?

Q16. How do cats feel when you make direct eye contact with them?

A15. Play

 ANSWERS

A16. Threatened

Q17. What do cats generally do to end a confrontation with another animal?

 QUESTIONS

Q18. How are cats feeling when they approach someone with a straight, vibrating tail?

A17. Yawn

 ANSWERS

A18. Happy

Q19. When a cat sticks his butt in your face, it's a gesture of _____.

 QUESTIONS

Q20. How are cats feeling when they put their whiskers back?

A19. Friendship

 ANSWERS

A20. Scared

Q21. What word is meant to describe cats grooming other cats?

 QUESTIONS

Q22. Pet cats like to sleep on things that smell like their _____.

A21. Allgrooming

 ANSWERS

A22. Owners

Q23. What kind of aromatic scent do cats really dislike?

Q24. How many cats did Abraham Lincoln have living in the White House?

A23. Citrus scents

 ANSWERS

A24. Four

Q25. What was Bill Clinton's pet cat's name?

 QUESTIONS

Q26. In which state in the US is there a cat named Stubbs who is a district mayor?

A25. Socks

 ANSWERS

A26. Alaska

Q27. A cat has the same learning ability as a human child of what age?

Q28. What is the word to describe a group of kittens?

A27. 2-3 years

 ANSWERS

A28. Kindle

Q29. What are cat breeders called?

 QUESTIONS

Q30. How many species of animals have cats contributed to the extinction of?

A29. Catteries

 ANSWERS

A30. 33

Q31. Cats were first brought to the Americas in colonial times to get rid of what?

 QUESTIONS

Q32. When was the first known cat video recorded?

A31. Rodents

 ANSWERS

A32. 1894

Q33. What colour eyes are cats born with?

 QUESTIONS

Q34. What is the word for a cat kneading the ground?

A33. Blue

 ANSWERS

A34. Snurgling

Q35. What is the normal body temperature of cat in Fahrenheit?

 QUESTIONS

Q36. What type of cat breed generally does not have a tail?

A35. 102 degrees Fahrenheit

 ANSWERS

A36. Manx Cat

Q37. What type of cat breed has the longest fur?

 QUESTIONS

Q38. Which country in the world has the highest cat per capita?

A37. Persian Cat

 ANSWERS

A38. New Zealand

Q39. What is the word describing a group of cats?

 QUESTIONS

Q40. What is the word describing a phobia of cats?

A39. Clowder

 ANSWERS

A40. Ailurophobia

Q41. What is the name of the cat in Garfield & Friends comic?

 QUESTIONS

Q42. What is the fastest that a house cat can run in miles per hour?

A41. Odie

 ANSWERS

A42. 30 miles per hour

Q43. What was the name of the first cat to travel to space?

 QUESTIONS

Q44. What type of cat breed is generally of the smallest size?

A43. Felicette

 ANSWERS

A44. Singapura

Q45. Which Catholic Pope declared cats as evil?

 QUESTIONS

Q46. What was the world's oldest cat called?

A45. Pope Innocent VIII

 ANSWERS

A46. Creme Puff

Q47. What age did the world's oldest cat live to?

 QUESTIONS

Q48. How many whiskers does an average cat have?

A47. 38 years

 ANSWERS

A48. 24

Q49. From how many stories can a cat fall without dying?

 QUESTIONS

Q50. What is the first ever recorded cartoon cat character?

A49. Any height

 ANSWERS

A50. Felix the Cat

Q51. How were people punished in ancient Egypt for smuggling a cat out of the country?

 QUESTIONS

Q52. What is the name for a female cat?

A51. Death penalty

 ANSWERS

A52. Molly

Q53. What is the biggest creature in the cat family?

 QUESTIONS

Q54. When was the animated series of Tom and Jerry created?

A53. Siberian tiger

 ANSWERS

A54. 1940

Q55. What was Tom's original debut name in the cartoon series Tom and Jerry?

 QUESTIONS

Q56. How many different types of sounds can a cat make?

A55. Jasper

 ANSWERS

A56. 100

Q57. Who created the American comic strip Garfield?

 QUESTIONS

Q58. What day of the week does Garfield hate?

A57. Jim Davis

 ANSWERS

A58. Monday

Q59. What type of cat is Garfield?

 QUESTIONS

Q60. Which was the first country to send a cat to space?

A59. Tabby cat

 ANSWERS

A60. France

Q61. How many people, on average, are bitten by cats every year in the United States?

Q62. Approximately how fast does the heart of a cat beat?

A61. 40,000

 ANSWERS

A62. 160-240 beats per minute

Q63. Which big cat is not able to retract its claws?

 QUESTIONS

Q64. What is the name of the largest living cat?

A63. Cheetah

 ANSWERS

A64. Hercules

Q65. What is a cross breed between a tiger and lion called?

 QUESTIONS

Q66. What is the name of the heaviest recorded house cat?

A65. Liger

 ANSWERS

A66. Himmy

Q67. What is the record for highest number of tricks completed by a pet cat in one minute?

 QUESTIONS

Q68. What is the record for the most toes on a cat?

A67. 20

 ANSWERS

A68. 28

Q69. What is the name of the pet cat with the long fur ever recorded?

 QUESTIONS

Q70. What food item is on the body of the internet meme Nyan Cat?

A69. Colonel Meow

 ANSWERS

A70. Pop-Tart

Q71. What was the rank of the video Nyan Cat among most viewed YouTube videos in 2011?

 QUESTIONS

Q72. Approximately how many views did the viral video Nyan Cat have?

A71. 5

 ANSWERS

A72. 170 million

Q73. What is a cat's knee known as?

 QUESTIONS

Q74. How long does it take for a kitten to develop a full set of teeth?

A73. Stifle

 ANSWERS

A74. 8 weeks

Q75. What is the highest frequency a cat can hear?

 QUESTIONS

Q76. A cat's tongue has a ____ surface with small barbs.

A75. 60,000 Hz

 ANSWERS

A76. Rough

Q77. Instead of sweating like humans, how do cats release excess body heat?

 QUESTIONS

Q78. What cat breed is also known as Aby-grabbys?

A77. Panting

 ANSWERS

A78. Abyssinian Cat

Q79. What cat breed has an orange coat and is a hybrid of a domestic cat and the wild Asian Leopard Cat?

 QUESTIONS

Q80. Which cat breed resulted from the cross of the Siamese and the Copper cat?

A79. Bengal Cat

 ANSWERS

A80. Burmese Cat

Q81. Which cat breed was bred to resemble the black leopard found in India?

Q82. Which cat breed is also known as the Himmie?

A81. Bombay Cat

 ANSWERS

A82. Himalayan Cat

Q83. What was the first Himmie kitten named?

 QUESTIONS

Q84. Which cat breed originates from ancient Mesopotamia?

A83. Newton's Debutante

 ANSWERS

A84. Persian Cat

Q85. Which cat breed is named for the way they collapse limply into the arms of anyone holding them?

 QUESTIONS

Q86. Which cat breed is also known as "little lions of love"?

A85. Ragdoll Cat

 ANSWERS

A86. Singapura Cat

Q87. Which cat breed often features in Russian fairy tales, folktales, and children's books?

Q88. Which cat breed was bred to resemble wild tigers in a domestic environment?

A87. Siberian Cat

 ANSWERS

A88. Toyger Cat

Q89. Which cat breed is said to have originated in the Isle of Mann?

 QUESTIONS

Q90. Which cat breed is one of mystery and legend, and revered as a sacred cat in Myanmar?

A89. Manx Cat

 ANSWERS

A90. Birman Cat

Q91. How many hours does a kitten sleep every day on average?

 QUESTIONS

Q92. Cats sleep many hours during the day to recharge their body for what activity?

A91. 20 hours

 ANSWERS

A92. Hunting

Q93. What is the word used to describe a short sleep similar to the ones cat have?

 QUESTIONS

Q94. How much money did the richest cat in the world have?

A93. A catnap

A94. 7 million pounds

Q95. What was the richest cat in the world called?

Q96. Which famous scientist who postulated gravity is also believed to have invented the cat door?

A95. Blackie

 ANSWERS

A96. Sir Isaac Newton

Q97. What would ancient Egyptians shave off when their cats died?

 QUESTIONS

Q98. House cats share almost 96% of their genetic makeup with which other animal?

A97. Eyebrows

 ANSWERS

A98. Tigers

Q99. What is the name of the cat who holds the record for the most tricks performed by a cat in 1 minute?

 QUESTIONS

Q100. What is the name of the cat to hold the record of the loudest recorded purr?

A99. Didga

 ANSWERS

A100. Merlin